For Emily & Max

Many thanks to Emily Eibel, Erica Rand Silverman and Tara Walker and her team at Tundra — especially Sophie Paas-Lang, Margot Blankier and Katelyn Chan — for their guidance, encouragement and support.

Special thanks to my models, Maxwell Awan and Wolfy & Snorri.

Tundra Books, an imprint of Tundra Book Group, a division of Penguin Random House of Canada Limited

Library and Archives Canada Cataloguing in Publication

Title: Strum and drum / Jashar Awan.
Names: Awan, Jashar, author, illustrator.
Identifiers: Canadiana (print) 20210343044 | Canadiana (ebook) 20210343087 |
ISBN 9780735272392 (hardcover) | ISBN 9780735272408 (EPUB)
Classification: LCC PZ7.1.A93 Str 2022 | DDC j813/.6—dc23

Published simultaneously in the United States of America by Tundra Books of Northern New York, an imprint of Tundra Book Group, a division of Penguin Random House of Canada Limited

Library of Congress Control Number: 2021948359

Edited by Tara Walker with assistance from Margot Blankier
Designed by Sophie Paas-Lang
The artwork in this book was created using pencil, chalk, Adobe Creative Suite and visions of sugar plums.
The text was set in Aldine.

Printed in China

www.penguinrandomhouse.ca

1   2   3   4   5   26   25   24   23   22

Penguin
Random House
tundra | TUNDRA BOOKS

STRUM & DRUM

A Merry Little Quest

Jashar Awan

tundra

The night was
silent and still.

Until . . .

Strum strummed his guitar and
Drum drummed her drum.

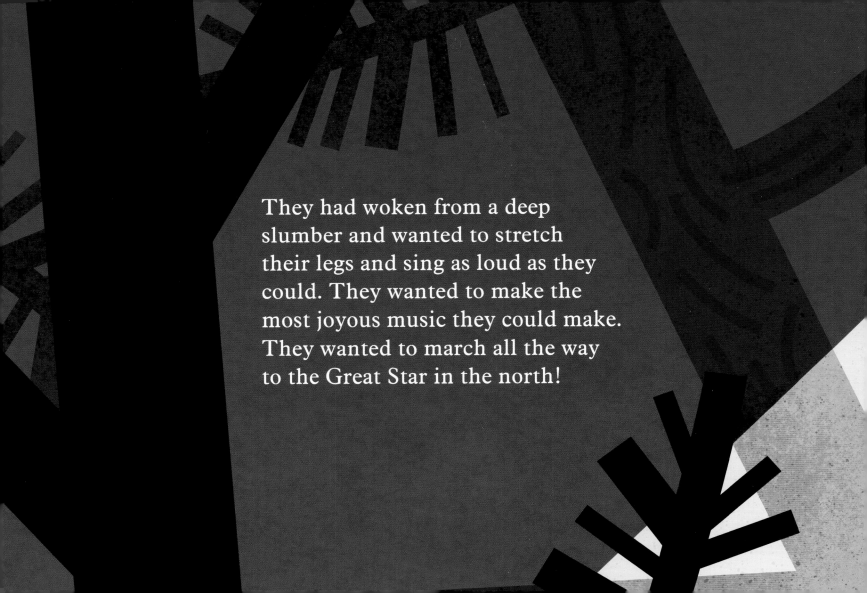

They had woken from a deep slumber and wanted to stretch their legs and sing as loud as they could. They wanted to make the most joyous music they could make. They wanted to march all the way to the Great Star in the north!

And that is exactly what they did . . .

strumming and drumming as they went.

The way was lit with lanterns that would flicker
and snuff out and then relight all on their own.

When the way was blocked by a silver waterfall . . .

Strum and Drum leapt through it . . .

Above their heads, bubbles of glass floated without a pop.

They followed the bubbles to a
small house in the distance . . .

. . . that remained a small house on a closer look.

They knocked, but no one was home.

When Strum and Drum became peckish, they gobbled up the sweets they found along the way and even tasted a single savory snack.

The mushrooms were relieved to have gone unnoticed.

The polar bear and penguins
in the woods, however, were
harder to miss.

But Strum and Drum marched along,
making their merry sound until a
whisper stopped them in their tracks.

What are
you doing?

the voice asked.

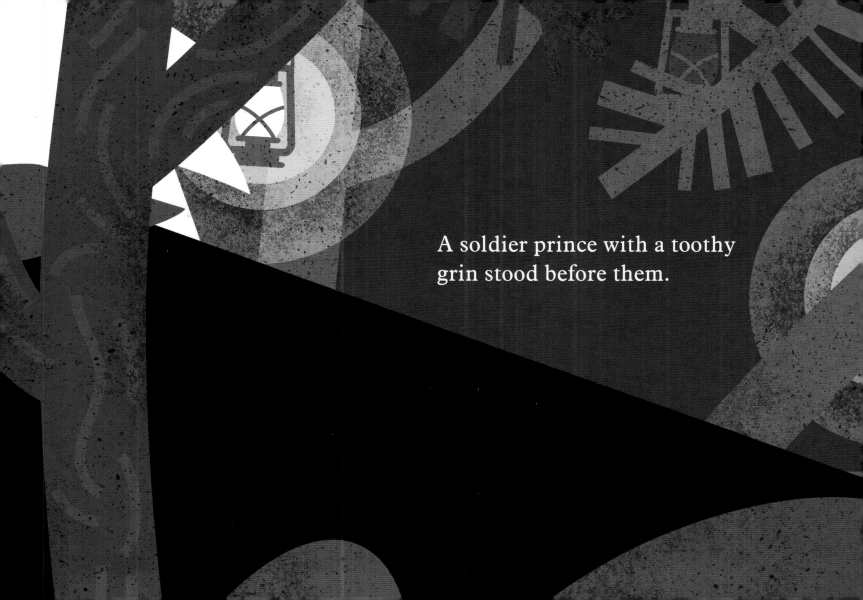

A soldier prince with a toothy
grin stood before them.

The soldier prince with the toothy grin said

I'll forgive you because you're so young. But in these woods, we have a saying . . .

Stay silent and still — or the beast with green eyes will catch you, it will.

A chorus of silent singers
nodded in agreement.

Even the snowflakes, which hung in the air and never gathered underfoot, quietly agreed.

But above the woods, the Great Star
still shone bright. The two gave each
other a smile and marched on . . .

strumming and drumming
as they went.

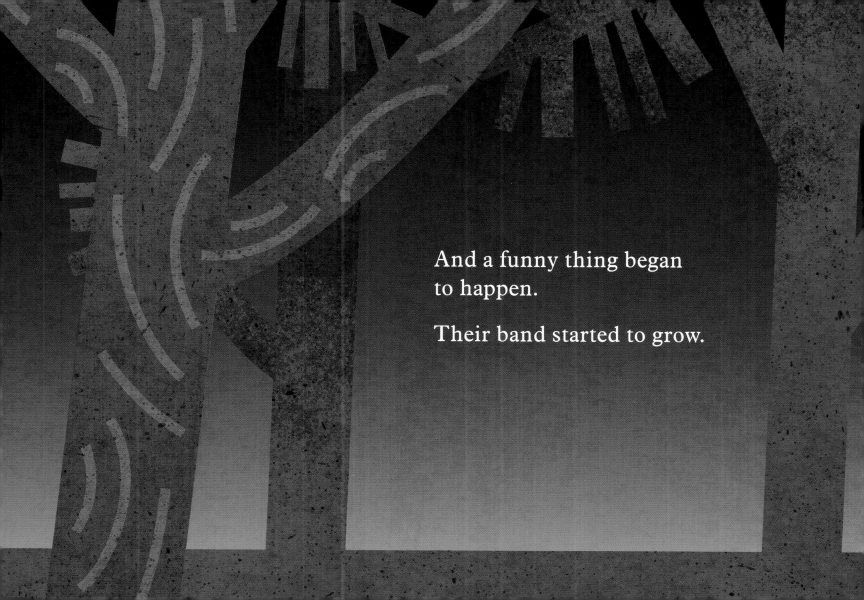

And a funny thing began
to happen.

Their band started to grow.

And grow.

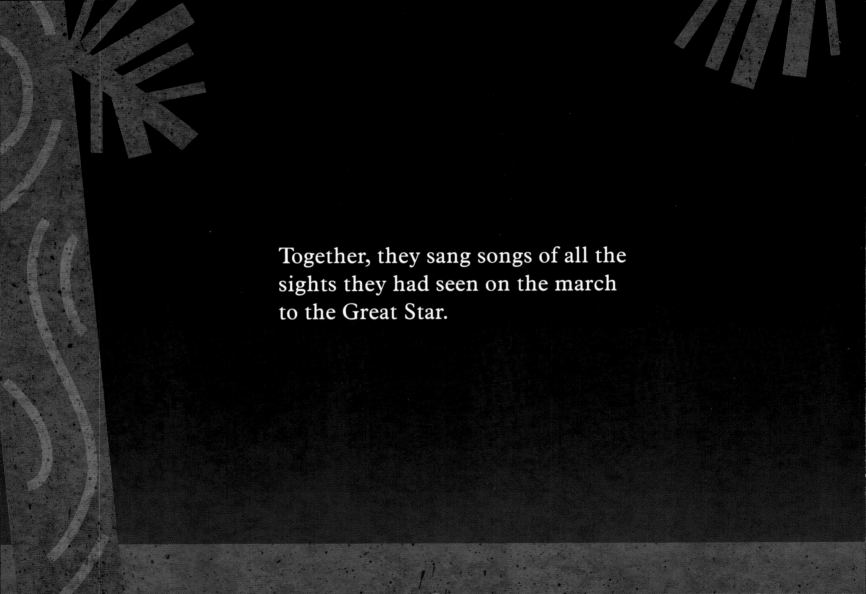

Together, they sang songs of all the
sights they had seen on the march
to the Great Star.

And they, too,
had not gone unseen.

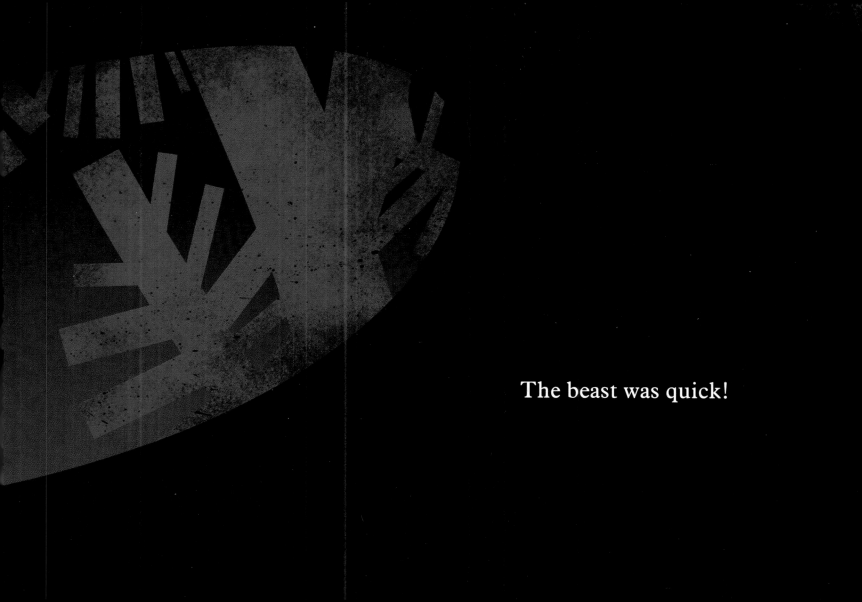

The beast was quick!

Strum and Drum went
tumbling through the air . . .

out of the woods and away
from all they had known.

A boy holding a glass of milk and
a plate of cookies stood over them.

"Bad cat!" he said.

The cat looked up innocently
and meowed in its own defense.

The boy placed Strum and Drum back
on the tree as high as he could reach.

"Mittens won't bother you up here,"
he promised.

As the boy shuffled off to bed,
the night was silent and still.

Until . . .

Strum strummed his guitar

and Drum drummed her drum.